Hot Wife Game - A Victorian England Hotwife Wife Watching Romance Novel

Hot Wife In Victorian England, Volume 1

Karly Violet

Published by Karly Violet, 2024.

Chapter One: Entirely Thankful

There have been many days when I have been proud of Lydia. For a start, she so willingly gave up her hand to put into mine as my beautiful wife. How she has found strength to contend with the likes of me is a divine mystery. However, she causes me joy in so many other ways from day to day, and it is for this reason I grow more fond of her by the moment. Today of all days, she has decided to give me the honour of enjoying her mother's recipe for egg fritters and pear butter.

"Here you are, my sweet Lewis," my wife says while smiling sweetly at me. She sits down on the other side of our small table before sitting and waiting for me to take a bite.

"You will not have any?" I ask. "Surely it is good enough for you as well, Lydia?"

"It is very fine," she promises, "But you know that a lady must not eat before noon."

Shaking my head, I say to her, "That is completely ridiculous. There is nothing ladylike about causing yourself to starve, Lydia! Please, have some with me."

Her eyes look down at the meal on my plate. "That was all the eggs I could muster for now."

"What?" I look toward the stove and shake my head. "I cannot eat this without making certain you have what you need. Please at least share this with me."

Lydia nods her head and quietly goes to fetch another fork. She then joins me at the table, moving her chair against mine, so that we can eat together."

"It is very good," I tell my wife after swallowing the first bite. "Why did you make only two eggs?"

She sighs. "We did not have any more. Unfortunately, we are without money at the moment, Lewis. When you left last week to complete your exams, the seamstress came by and told me she would have no new work for me." Lydia turns her eyes away as she digs at one of the eggs with her fork. It seems her appetite might not be as it should be at the moment due to the stress of losing the needed income.

"You should have told me," I reply softly. "My love, I could have taken on work over the weekend. The butcher is always in need of another set of hands to help him with the hogs."

"And you would have come home smelly and too tired for me yesterday," she says with a frown. "You are to be a solicitor, and that will help to bring our fortunes up somewhat. We must only be patient."

Frowning, I tell her, "I will not eat without you, Lydia. You know that about me. For many years I lived on a farm while growing up, and my mother taught me to honour a woman, no matter the cost. You are my wife and I will protect you from all things, no matter their origin."

My wife turns to me and kisses me on the cheek before pushing the half-eaten egg toward my side of the plate. "You must eat to remain strong today. Remember, this is your very first day as a solicitor in training, and I do not want you to feel faint from not eating, Lewis."

"I will not faint. Lydia, you know I cannot allow you to go without. This is my motivation to become a solicitor, after all."

Though only twenty-five years of age, I did not begin my life in university. No, I first struggled to work on local farms as a handyman of sorts. However, this life often did not pay well and it sometimes required work that was not suitable for my wife's needs. We agreed that I would use my inheritance from my grandfather's small estate to pay for my university education, and it was barely enough to do so. However, I have completed my formal training and must now go through an apprenticeship to gain my practising certificate.

"You have worked very hard, Lewis. I owe you so much." She reaches for me and puts her arm around me where I sit. "You will not forget me after becoming a famous Southampton solicitor, will you?"

I laugh. "You know I cannot live apart from you for more than a day or two. My body would soon collapse into itself and I would cease to exist. Everything of any value in this world is nothing compared to you."

Lydia smiles, her cheeks turning bright red as she looks away from me. It is one of the most endearing features about my young wife that I have come to know. She is, by her very nature, a shy creature. There are many times when I must step forward and become her advocate in the midst of those who my wife feels are attempting to belittle or discourage her. As a matter of fact, I will become an angry tiger and roar at any who I feel are abusing the gentle nature of my dear Lydia. She deserves only the fittest compliments or encouragement, and I will not allow her to become someone else's vessel for abuse.

"You are everything to me as well, my dearest husband. It has been my prayer that the solicitors at the office will treat you fairly."

"You remember Phineas Hutchins, do you not? He and his cousin James are the proprietors. They have offered to hone my knowledge and to help me build a rapport with the courts. It is the most important part of my education to date, Lydia."

"I know," she giggles. "I am so very proud of all you have accomplished, my love." Reaching down, she takes a small scoop of the breakfast and places it inside her mouth. "You must eat. If I must eat to see it done, then I will."

Smiling, I wink at her before picking up my own fork. For the next few minutes, we enjoy the food as well as a cup of stout, black coffee. After finishing, I quickly prepare my satchel and walk out the door to go to the horse tied to a post. Though I do not own the horse, a neighbor nearby has offered the old nag so that I might be able to ride the three miles to my new position in Southampton. Thankfully, the Hutchins's have made arrangements for me to leave the horse at a livery stable near their office each day.

"I will see you shortly before dark, Lydia," I tell my wife before kissing her on the forehead. "If you prepare dinner, do not do so with the intent that I will be the only one eating. If you do not eat, I do not eat. That is a new law within our home."

"And the solicitor must know the law," she quips whilst raising an eyebrow.

"I do." I kiss her again before turning to get atop the horse. After settling into the saddle, I give her a quick tap with my heels into her side and off we go down the road toward Southampton proper.

Though my wife worries for me, I worry as much for her. She will almost always give up her own comforts for mine, but I cannot allow her to continue in this vein. No, I must protect her, no matter the cost to me.

Chapter Two: Getting to Work

As I walk into the office of Hutchins & Hutchins, I find myself in awe of my quaint surroundings. The office, located between a bakery and a mercantile, is not large by any means. Relatively unassuming, it does not shout to me the social standing of either man who works here. Instead, it feels somewhat homey to me, though I grew up on a farm and scratched my way through university.

"Good morning, Mr. Dabney," James Hutchins says to me as she approaches with a hand extended. I take it to shake as he asks, "How was your ride this morning?"

"It was fair," I reply with a smile. "The sun is out and the dew is not as thick."

"Aye, the weather will be a concern for you, I am certain," he tells me. "We shall determine what must be done to keep you from becoming soaked from Southampton's rains."

"This is the new lad, then?" Another man says as he approaches and offers me his hand as well. "Phineas Hutchins."

"Lewis Dabney," I reply. "I do believe we have met before, but I was only seventeen or so at the time."

"Ah, the younger brother of Samuel. He is a good man, your brother."

"We are of the same opinion," I say with a nod and smile. "He sends you both glad tidings from Sussex."

"But, you do reside much closer, I hope?" Phineas asks.

"I do, sir. Only three miles west of this place, to be precise. An old mare brings me here today."

"A mare?" James raises his eyebrows. "Certainly we will need to address this soon, Mr. Dabney. We cannot have one of our solicitors riding an old mare through the early morning rains this time of year." He shakes his head and I feel a tinge of embarrassment for having to borrow the old horse to arrive here. I discussed with James that I would be traveling by horse, but I did not tell him it would be an old mare.

"And you are married, sir?" Phineas asks.

"I am," I answer him. "My wife Lydia sends her regards." I lift a tin full of freshly baked biscuits. "These are for the two of you, gentlemen. She would not allow me to leave the house this morning without bringing them."

How very considerate," James says with a smile as he reaches out and takes the tin from my hands. "We should enjoy some hot tea later along with these biscuits. However, it would be prudent to first see where you shall be working in our office for the next six months, sir." He motions one hand toward a desk situated in the corner of the room outside one of the two offices. As I make my way to it, I notice there are several things situated for my use upon its top.

"You have a pen as well as pencils here," James Hutchins tells me, "And here is some paper. Along the edge of the desk are receptacles for the case work we will be giving you on occasion, and this is where you have a small lantern for any additional lighting you might require."

"And this?" I point toward a fine leather satchel in the chair.

"'Tis yours," James replies with a wide smile. "Phineas and I felt you should have a fine solicitor's satchel for your beginnings. What do you think?"

I look down at the very worn satchel still in my hand that I was able to borrow from an old physician down the road from me. Suddenly, a feeling of great pride rode across my face as I took a deep breath and realized I would now have the makings of a solicitor, if only by appearance.

"Thank you dearly for these things," I say to the cousins. "You are much more generous than I deserve."

Phineas puts a hand upon my shoulder. "Surely a man in our profession must be fitted for such. You cannot go before a magistrate with a worn satchel, Mr. Dabney. It would be somewhat unseemly."

"I understand completely," I reply. "Thank you very much."

"Come this way, sir," James says to me. I follow him to his office and Phineas follows just behind me. After we enter, we all sit down and James puts his hands together on top of his desk. "So, you are to be gaining your practising certificate in six months, then. What are we to have you do to earn such a prestigious honour?"

"I am very ready to go to work at your leisure, sir," I tell him. "As a new apprentice in the law, I have already been in court with another solicitor to glean whatever I might from him."

"Tony Brockton," James says as he smiles. "A very fine solicitor, indeed. 'Tis a good thing you have seen such a master of the arts we practise."

"He is indeed," Phineas agrees. "I have had the good fortune of working alongside the man a time or two over the years. His mind is quick and sharp."

"I have been blessed to be around him for some time. It was Mr. Brockton who offered a letter to the university where I attended to study the law."

"He holds sway," James agrees. "I have seen him woo the Crown's solicitors into giving his clients their way on more than one occasion. Should I need someone to defend me before the courts, I would ask him."

"Aye? And am I no longer your greatest hope?" his cousin muses.

"Phineas, you know as well as I that I find you completely immaculate within your sense of the judiciary. Still yet, there is a readiness on Mr. Brockton's part to open up the gates of hell upon a client's accusers."

We all laugh together, the heartiness of the amusement filling my soul with gladness. Though I have known these two men before, James more so than Phineas, I was uncertain how difficult they might see to my introduction into their world. After all, there are many solicitors who are quick to make short work of newcomers, no matter their intelligence or mental aptitude. The profession is one that is close-knit and difficult to break into as an outside. I am glad to have both of the other men in this room willing to support me as I continue my training.

"So, we should expect to have dinner, then? Friday evening?" Phineas looks over at me. "It has been some time since we met before, and I have not had the same opportunity as my cousin to come to know you as I should. My wife, Adelia, should be happy enough to make your acquaintance, as well as that of your wife."

"Lydia would be most pleased to meet Mrs. Hutchins."

My mind turns to what my wife said to me just three days before now. We are to see her parents this Saturday and to spend the night before returning Sunday. Unfortunately, I cannot refuse an invitation to enjoy dinner with one of my two employers. Not during the first week. So, I can only agree to do as asked by Phineas and accept his invitation.

"What time, then?" I ask.

"Seven o'clock on Friday evening, Mr. Dabney."

"Lewis, if you please," I say to him. "It will be our honour to attend dinner at your home on Friday."

"Excellent!" Phineas smiles widely as he looks over at his cousin. "I must see to work, unless you need me here whilst discussing the terms, James."

James shakes his head. "I believe we can manage quite well without you, sir."

Phineas stands from his seat and offers a slight head bow to us before leaving James's office to go to his own. I turn my eyes back to the other Mr. Hutchins and take a breath as I await his next instruction.

"There is a court case that I have given you to whet your appetite upon such things," James begins as he looks at a file before handing it to me. "There is a man who has been arrested for vagrancy. His name is Colin O'Toole."

"Vagrancy? Where?"

"The courthouse steps," James answers while sighing. "Poor Colin has pestered one too many justices and solicitors and has found himself owing some money for fines due to vagrancy. So, he shall appear before the Right Honourable Marshall Goodwin on Tuesday from next."

"Surely he must pay," I say as I look at the file. "There is little to do here if the man is guilty as charged."

"Aye, that is easy to accept in such cases, Lewis. However, Phineas and I are quick to defend such men nonetheless. Colin is not within his faculties and therefore must be given some reprieve by the magistrate."

"Would he listen to someone like me?" I ask. "I have been told the magistrates in Southampton are amongst the strictest when it comes to who shall speak to them in open court."

"You are allowed to speak," James replies. "It might not make happy some of the older magistrates, but they surely must follow the law and the law allows for an apprentice solicitor to speak on behalf of the indigent."

"Indigent?" I shake my head. "The vagrant has no money?"

"No, he does not. And do not refer to him thusly before a court," James warns me. "Most magistrates will attempt to use the words of younger solicitors against them."

"Understood," I answer. "And so, this man, Mr. O'Toole. Do I see him in the streets or will he come here to meet with me?"

"He knows to come to our office," he replies. "Whether the man will or not remains to be seen, however. Phineas and I have seen the man for the last month." James frowns, the depth of the furrow in his eyebrows allowing a glimpse into his concern for the man.

"Where might one fine him?" I ask. "Surely I might see him near the court or along some street adjacent."

"Mr. O'Toole is a slight man, no taller than most women, with greying hair and a disheveled appearance. His eyes are a cold steely sort, framed by bushy eyebrows that are quite unkempt. Surely if you see this man, you would know him."

"Might I smell him?" I ask.

"Smell him? Do you take time to gather the scents of others, Lewis?"

I chuckle. "I grew up on a farm, sir. Aromas were of great importance there so that we might have a better sense of what was happening amongst our livestock."

"Ah. I see your point." James nods his head. "The man has likely not bathed in a year or more. The stink upon him should be quite great."

"Right. I will keep my eyes and nose at attention as I walk the streets later, Mr. Hutchins."

"Call me James," he replies. "It would be much better if we all carry on a close understanding whilst working together, don't you agree?"

"Of course."

"Then off with you. Please take the folder with you and study it at your desk. Should you have questions, please address either of us with them."

"I will, thank you sir." Standing to my feet, I turn to leave his office. Soon, I am at my new desk where I am able to open the folder and study the information within a bit closer than before. Colin O'Toole appears to be a man who is in considerable need, lacking even the basic necessities for life. Those inside the court may not be able to see this so clearly, but I can. I have lived a difficult life for the last twenty-five years and hope to do more than continue mucking out the stalls on local farmers' farms.

Chapter Three: Untenable Position

14

"No, Lewis! You must tell them you cannot do this!" Lydia glares at me from across our small kitchen table while pursing her lips tightly together. "We cannot go on Friday evening to Mr. Hutchin's house. My parents expect that we shall arrive in Sussex by train."

I take a breath, knowing very well that I will need to work hard to convince my dear wife of the importance of such things.

"My love, I could not refuse such a generous offer to attend for dinner. Mr. Hutchins, Phineas, says his wife is very eager to meet you on Friday. They have already planned for our arrival."

"My mother and father have planned as well," she argues. "Do you expect that I will simply tell them we will not come to their house?"

"Please, Lydia. I need to show an eagerness to do as they ask in the beginning. As I gain their favour, I will be in a better position to make such requests. Also, we do not have friends."

Her eyes suddenly turn to look into mine. "Are you suggesting I am the culprit behind such a curse, Lewis?"

"I am not," I answer.

"You most certainly are. You have never accepted that I feel painfully inadequate around those of social standing, husband. I have seen you grow tired of my silly concerns."

"Your concerns are not silly," I reply. "Please do not say so, Lydia."

"Lewis, it is obvious you are not pleased with me. Whenever we are asked to attend a dinner with someone, you immediately agree when I do not."

"You always refuse, Lydia," I say accusatorily. "I know you have concerns that fill you with angst, but surely we must exercise them from you by doing the very thing you dislike."

She shakes her head. "I do not need to socialize with the likes of the Hutchins's."

"But, you do," I argue. "We both do if I am to see my new profession grow. My love, I need to become one of them, and I cannot do that without you."

My wife, angry enough already, seems to become even angrier as she shakes her head slowly. We have had the same argument many times before, only upon different premises. She is very self-observant whenever it comes to the hardships she has faced due to her painful shyness, and this had not abated since we married. Unfortunately, shyness is not helpful to either of us as I begin to work as a solicitor.

Lydia stands up from her seat and walks over to a window. While looking outside, she asks, "Would you have me perform for them, Lewis? Shall I dance and sing for the Lord and Lady of the house?"

"They are not nobility," I tell her. "Neither are called Lord or Lady."

"But, they must feel themselves so called. They have the money behind it."

I laugh. "You have too much time to think through such things. My love, why do you worry so?" Standing to my feet, I make my way to her at the window.

"I cannot do this, Lewis. I do not know them and you know I do not like dining with those I do not know."

Pulling Lydia to me, we kiss passionately, our hands moving along each other's bodies. There is a strong attraction between the two of us, and it is apparent as we begin to move aggressively with each other. Pulling at my wife, I take her to the bedroom and push her to the bed. She smiles just before I pull up her dress and kiss her legs. The sweet giggles that erupt from her lips urge me to move further up her soft thigh to the point of finding her sweet, bushy quim. Nestling my lips against her wet valley, my tongue easily finds its target.

Suddenly, my wife pushes me away from her. "Lewis!"

"My dear," I say with surprise.

"You know we do not do such things." Lydia pulls her dress down to cover her bushy grove.

"We are married," I complain while shaking my head. "Are we not married, my love? You should not refuse me."

Angrily, she retorts, "I do not refuse you, husband. I offer you my body, but only in the most righteous context. We do not put our faces into each other's nethers."

"This is not a fair thing you do to me."

"We were agreed before we took our vows, Lewis. You knew when you awaited me at the altar that I would not allow such unholy things to be done upon me."

"In what way is it unholy?" I plead with her. "There is nothing in the holy scriptures that forbids a married couple from enjoying each other completely. We are pledged to each other, body and soul, are we not?"

"You are not to spill your seed, Lewis. This is what we have both been taught in church."

"I would not spill my seed to simply taste of you, though. Why I cannot enjoy such a wonderful thing does not make sense." Taking a long breath, I add, "You would have me a minister if I would acquiesce to such a thing."

I speak only the truth when accusing my wife of as much. From her own lips, she has attempted in the past to convince me that my calling is to the church and I should prepare in this way. Becoming a solicitor was something I had wished to do, and though Lydia has been somewhat supportive, she is not completely happy. She believes that the social standing of those in the church supersedes that of those who are solicitors, and therefore would be preferable. In this we have disagreed many times.

"You cannot put your face there," she says again very firmly. "I will not do the same for you, either."

My face turns red as I turn and go back to the bed and have a seat. How do I argue with a woman who has decided that to enjoy each other fully is a sin? We are married and all I ask is that we might enjoy each other in every way possible. It is not as if I have asked her to become a whore.

"You are sometimes cold toward me, Lydia. Then you are also unwilling to help me seal my relationship with those who compensate me as a new solicitor. It will be a great slap upon my own face should I go to Phineas Hutchins and tell him we will not come to his home this coming Friday evening. You will apparently have your way on things no matter the circumstances."

There is a long silence in the room between us as Lydia stares at me. She does not know what to say at first, as I have spoken only the truth to her. In marriage, we have been true partners in so few things up until now. It is time for my wife to begin thinking of what I must do as a solicitor instead of seeking for some way to make her own life completely comfortable for her. If she will not at least allow me to taste her musky quim, she must give in to my request for us to go to dinner at the Hutchins's house.

"This will be difficult for me," she says softly. "I will send word to Momma and Papa that we will not come visit this weekend, Lewis. We will attend the dinner you have been invited to at the Hutchins's home." Lydia sits down beside me on the bed. "Do you truly hate me for refusing your advances? I do not wish to be so caustic, but you sometimes leave me no alternative, my sweet husband." She puts her hand on my face and smiles sweetly.

"You do not wish to give in to me completely. When you say that you told me as much before we married, you were correct. I suppose I have continued to hope that you would give me more than you have, Lydia. However, that hope is fading quickly."

There is a sad expression on her face as she simply looks back at me. My wife understands that I am not happy with the lack of true intimacy between us, but she is unwavering in her rejection of the oral arts. Cunnilingus and fellatio are not the sorts of things she finds particularly attractive. Her mother would likely see such a thing as a hideous expression of hedonism.

"I am sorry you are so disappointed with me, Lewis," Lydia replies. "You have been patient with me for so long, but I can see that you have finally begun to realize the wife you have married."

"I have known to whom I am married since saying my vows," I tell her. "For some time I have hoped against hope that you might be accepting of my advances, though."

"We may have intimate relations, Lewis. We have done as much for the entirety of our marriage, have we not? Why do you need to do such disgusting things to me? Surely you do not wish to be married to a harlot?"

Standing once again, I tell her, "We are married, and as your husband I have been asking for more of you in bed. You do not wish to give me that which I ask, and I must come to accept your unwillingness to do so. I cannot promise that I will find it quite as satisfying as you do." Turning, I walk to the doorway before looking back for a moment to see the same sad expression on her face. Seeing that there is little more I can say to her, I turn around and walk back into the kitchen and out through a side door of the house.

The sun, finally setting in the west, leaves an orange haze over the horizon that is at the same time exciting as it is soothing. There are things in my life I must use to fill the absence of true intimacy with my shy wife. Thankfully the setting sun nor the rising moon refuse my request to look upon them. Their nakedness must stand in place of Lydia's soft quim fur upon my face. No matter what I say, she will not give in, and I cannot force my will upon her. I will not. The sort of gentleman I am will never allow me to take what I want from my wife. Unlike other husbands, I will simply allow my suffering in silence for the sake of the one I love deeply. If only she loved me enough to offer her entire body to me at my whim.

Chapter Four: Plain Speak

The tenor of the room is not what I had hoped it would be as we sit and have drinks with Phineas and Adelia Hutchins. They have been incredibly gracious to the both of us, serving a dinner worthy of nobility rather than a farmhand turned solicitor and his wife. Though such wonderful care from our hosts should give Lydia reason to be happy in their presence, she seems withdrawn and unwilling to interact.

"At any rate, we are quite pleased to have you with us, dear boy," Phineas says to me as he reaches over and pats me on the arm. The solicitor then takes a sip from his glass of wine before putting it onto a small table nearby.

"I am very pleased to be with you as well," I reply. "To be selected to take up the six-month position with you and your cousin is quite an honour."

"You came highly recommended," Phineas tells me. "Your professors were happy to lend their names to your application."

"They honour me as well."

"And what about you?" Adelia asks my wife. "How do you see all that has happened so far with your husband and his ambitions to become a solicitor?"

Lydia looks at her nervously as she moves her wine glass around on top of the little table. "I support Lewis in all things. Of course, I am very proud of him." She turns her eyes to look at me. "He deserves all the wonderful things he has been able to experience so far because of his study of the law."

"Certainly, but what about you, my dear?" Mrs. Hutchins presses her. "Do you find what he is doing exciting at all? Or would you prefer to remain out of conversations about such things with him?"

My wife smiles awkwardly, her eyes not making contact with the other woman in the room as she replies, "I am not a solicitor, so I do not understand such conversations. However, I am quite happy, I can assure you." Only now does her eyes briefly flutter toward Adelia.

The quiet in the room continues to gnaw at me as I look to my employer and ask, "What stories have you about your time as solicitor, Phineas? Perhaps there is one or two from which I might learn something?"

The other man's face brightens up as he says, "There are a few that are very interesting, in fact. One in particular would include a case I worked on just this last year for a rather rude chap named Hugo."

"Hugo?" I say with a chuckle. "His first or last name."

Phineas raises an eyebrow. "I'm not certain. He was unpleasant from the very beginning, whatever the case. It seems he did not feel he should have to wear a shirt in the presence of ladies along the road as he walked along. The constabulary stopped him and informed him of the decency laws in Southampton, and he told them to bugger off. That did not sit well with them, however," he laughs.

"He did not intend to clothe himself?" I ask while allowing a laugh to evade my own lips. "Was he free of his faculties?"

"Not so much, no. Hugo wished to declare that no matter the law concerning such things, he did not need to wear a shirt. He was allowed to bare his hideously hair chest and back while those around him should be forced to look upon his furriness. The ladies continued to complain and he soon found himself before the court."

"Did he become more pliant after he was subjected to authority?" I ask.

"He did not. You see, Hugo appeared in a very nice suit that had been offered by a friend for him to wear. Once Hugo was in court and gave his account of what had happened, the magistrate suggested he might be amenable to a simple fine as long as my client swore to dress completely from now on. Unfortunately, something snapped in the poor man's mind and he began to curse the magistrate. After being instructed to sit down and shut up, Hugo stripped off his clothes, every inch, and ran around the courtroom with nothing on but the hair he was growing like a thick wool blanket. The courtroom guards took the man into custody and he was remanded to the custody of the prison for a term of six months."

"No," I hear my wife say softly while covering her mouth. "How rude he was."

"Indeed," Phineas replies. "And ruder still, from what I was told after he was taken back to prepare for transport to the prison. "Every vile exhortation Hugo could summon was brought out to the waiting ears of those along the route. There were a variety of additional accusations leveled against the man, but none that I know were brought for formal charging."

"Lydia," Adelia says to her after being so quiet for the last few minutes. "Would you mind accompanying me to the parlor for a few minutes? There is something I would like to discuss, if your husband agrees?"

"Absolutely," I say while nodding at her. Though reticent to doing so, my wife stands to her feet and follows the other woman out of the library.

"Do not worry. My wife will be gentle with Lydia." He pauses before asking, "Has she been so reserved all her life?"

I sigh. "She has, but she does not mean it as an affront, sir."

"No affront taken, good man," Phineas replies with a smile. "Adelia has noticed this and probably wants to have some time to get to know Lydia better so that they might not be so uncomfortable together. This is a very good thing."

"I thank you and Mrs. Hutchins for such a kind nature. Coming tonight has been quite difficult for Lydia."

He raises an eyebrow. "What have you not told me?"

"It is nothing, sir."

"Please, do not hold back, Lewis. Was your wife less than happy to accompany you to dinner tonight?"

My heart races inside my chest as I realize the experienced solicitor has deduced the underlying problem in our visit this evening. Surely I might as well have told him upfront what the problem was instead of letting him discover it on his own.

"She had expected to visit her parents this weekend," I tell him. "Lydia is very close to her mother, so she thought it a slight on my part that I did not tell you this once the invite was extended to us."

"I see. So very sorry for interrupting your life in this way, Lewis."

"No, please, do not feel as if you have anything to do with this, sir. We are very happy to have come to enjoy dinner with you and your wife."

"Still, Lydia does not like me at the moment, does she?"

"Perhaps not. However, she will warm up to you, I swear it."

Phineas laughs and reaches for his glass of wine. "I recall my first dinner after accepting a soliciting position several years ago before my cousin and I established our own office. It was not as I had hoped it would be, but I did not have a wife at the time with whom to be concerned."

"When did you marry Lydia?"

"Last year, in October," he replies. "After too many years on my own, I finally found a woman who was strong enough to live with the many intricacies of my odd personality. We have since found a wonderful intimacy that has been quite fulfilling."

Shaking my head, I tell him, "That is lacking in my own marriage, I am afraid. Lydia is not convinced that anything besides straight missionary is abiding by the holy book."

Phineas nods his head. "She is a prude of sorts?"

"She is," I agree. "Though I love her dearly, sir. I am completely devoted to her in all ways, and I will never leave her."

"A good man you are," he replies. "There are too few good men in this day and age. So many are willing to leave their wives to simply enjoy the forbidden fruit of other women. It is not necessary to do such a thing."

"I will never leave her," I say again.

"That much is obvious. Perhaps over time you will find Lydia becoming more aligned with what it is that you want, Lewis. Give her time and continue to be her most steadfast defender. Gentle Ladies appreciate knowing that their husbands are always on their side and prepared to die for them."

Phineas gives me more wine to drink and we continue our conversation for a while before the women return to the room. Lydia is talking freely, though quietly, with Adelia after they return. I am happy to see the two of them getting along so well finally.

"She tells me you broke off a trip to see her parents, Lewis?" Adelia asks.

"Wife, please do not scold him," Phineas responds. "We have been speaking on this matter as well. It is often the view of those who are new to a position that they must heed all calls by their employers."

"Of course, but we could have easily rescheduled," Adelia replies. "I have apologized to Lydia and this will not happen again."

"It will not?" Phineas muses.

"No, it will not," his wife reiterates firmly.

Turning to look at me, Mr. Hutchins says, "We will be certain to ask the wives before we schedule any further meals together." He laughs whilst winking at me.

"Good. Then, we will all be very happy friends from now on." Adelia smiles warmly at Lydia before asking, "You shall both stay as our guest for the evening so that you will not have to make the journey home in the dark. There have been rumbles in the distance that mean rain very soon, anyway."

"It is very generous of you to offer us a warm bed, but we do have a carriage outside that is waiting on us," I reply.

"All can be taken care of," Phineas assures me. "Allow us to do what we must to keep you both safe for the evening." He nods toward a servant, who then turns and walks through the doorway out of the room.

"Please do not allow us to be any trouble," Lydia says to them.

"Nonsense. There is no trouble in seeing that you have a place to stay for the reason. We are friends, are we not?" Mrs. Hutchins pats my wife on the shoulder. "Besides, I would very much enjoy speaking further with you on another matter, if you are willing?" My wife nods her head. "Good."

"I will keep Mr. Dabney out of trouble, I swear it," Phineas chuckles. "We shall enjoy more to drink and perhaps a book or two in the library."

As I watch, Lydia leaves the room with Adelia. Seeing her so happy with another woman makes me very happy as I never thought such a thing possible. For a long time, my wife has complained of the terrible fear she has of speaking to those she does not know well, especially if she is made to speak to them without someone she knows present. With such extreme shyness, I have wondered if there would ever come a time when Lydia could function so freely with another. Having seen the proof of her new abilities, I am both satisfied and ecstatic. All I have ever wished for her is to have good friends, and it seems that my wish is now coming to fruition.

Chapter Five: Something Different

"Breakfast was very nice," I say to Lydia as our carriage travels along the road toward our home. "Phineas and Adelia were very gracious hosts."

"They were," my wife says while looking at me only briefly before turning her eyes back to her hands.

Since leaving this morning, I have made note of some changes within Lydia's character that have caused me to be concerned. Though she became more talkative with Mrs. Hutchins last evening and then spent more time with her early into the morning hours, my wife seems to now avoid being an active participant in a conversation. Why has she suddenly shifted in this way?

"Are you well?" I ask.

"Quite well," she replies. "Why would you ask such a thing?"

Shrugging my shoulders, I answer, "You are not quite yourself, my love. Did something happen last evening while you were with Adelia?"

Her eyes quickly turn to look into mine. "Nothing happened," she says quickly. "All is well."

"But, you were not with me for most of the night," I point out. "I woke at three o'clock this morning and your side of the bed was empty. Did you go somewhere?"

Lydia frowns. "I was simply speaking to Adelia about our life and what you and I do as interests."

"Interests?"

"Certainly. For example, I told her about how you enjoy working outdoors with your hands."

"Ah."

I was raised on a small farm and therefore spent a lot of time working with farm animals and crops. To this day, I continue to see doing so an important part of my life, even though I have now taken on the task of practising the law as a solicitor. Lydia certainly understands my allure to such things as she was also raised on a small farm with her parents.

"What did you do when you discovered I was missing?" my wife asks.

"Well, nothing. I believed you to either be using the water closet or to be with Mrs. Hutchins once again. You seemed quite willing to spend time with her before bed, anyway."

"I did," she agrees. "And you were very chummy with Mr. Hutchins as well. What did you talk about with him, Lewis?"

I raise an eyebrow. "We discussed politics as well as my growing duties at the office. They will give me more responsibility as I show them worthy of my talents. With more work will come great pay." Smiling, I add, "We will soon be able to afford leaving our current home for one closer to my work. It will be a much nicer house, Lydia. I promise." Reaching over, I take her hand into mine and kiss it. This causes a slight blush to ride across her face.

"You are too kind to me," she says with a quivering voice. "Surely you will see me so spoiled by your sweetness, Lewis." Lydia looks away from me, and my heart aches for whatever is bothering her.

"Tell me what it is," I plead with her. "What do you hide from me, sweetheart?"

"I hide nothing from you," she replies. Her eyes turn to look out the side window of the carriage. "The fields are very pretty here, are they not?"

I turn to look at them as well, confused as to why my wife would seek to change the subject of our conversation so quickly.

"They are lovely, as are you."

"Do not speak so well of me." Her face turns bright red once more. Why does she seem so concerned about my adulation toward her? Have I embarrassed her sense of modesty with my terrible tongue?

"I have no one else I can speak better of," I inform Lydia as I smile again. "You are beyond all things for me, and I believe our hosts saw that last evening. We were very well represented by your willingness to engage with Adelia."

My wife shakes her head and tells me, "Open your trousers, sir."

"My trousers?"

"Yes. Open them and show me your snake."

My cock begins to grow hard as I ask, "What are you about, woman?"

"Will you refuse to me that which I am owed?" Lydia asks coarsely. At this, I am not so certain how I should respond other than to allow her to have that which she requires. So, I open my trousers and pull out my hardening member.

My wife, her face still pink, bends over and takes my cock into her soft, wet mouth. I am completely shocked by her sudden willingness to take in my pecker after all these years of marriage. Before this moment, she had said many times that she would do no such thing as it was anathema to her religious beliefs. However, Lydia now suckles upon me as if I will deliver life-giving milk across her tongue.

"Lydia, why are you doing this?" I ask in between heavy breaths. "You swore you would not do such a thing to me."

Slowly lifting her head and drawing her lips along my cock, my wife says to me, "You have wished this for so long, have you not? If so, please allow me to pleasure you, husband. I insist." Lydia then goes back down and once again engulfs my hard pole with her soft, inviting mouth.

"My love," I moan as she sucks gently upon it. "Oh, Lydia. Your tongue is wonderful." There is a strange sensation at the tip of my manhood as my wife swirls her tongue upon the very tip of it. Her hands gripping my bollocks at the same time means that I will soon release my seed into her awaiting throat to be swallowed into her stomach. This sort of action at one time would have been called patently sacrilegious by my wife not so many days before. What has happened to her? Why does she now allow herself to spoil my seed into the back of her soft mouth?

Lydia grips my cock hard as she spends more time at the end of it. I grip tightly the seat on either side of me as she does so, and I wonder what has brought her to such a conclusion as to her willingness to make me so happy. There are many questions that continue to fill my head, but the sudden ejection of my seed into her mouth causes me to call out in ecstasy.

"Ohhhh...OOOHHHHH!!!" I spurt hard into her awaiting mouth, causing Lydia to gag a little upon my male cream.

"Ack...UUUTTT!"

"Aaahhhh...AAAHHHHH!!! OOOOHHHH!!!" Pulling at her head, I seat my cock deep inside the back of Lydia's throat as she receives each   shot   of   my   creamy   concoction. *"UUUUHHHH...UUUUUHHHH!!!"*

"Uutttt...uuuutttt..."

I finish inside her mouth before Lydia quickly pulse her lips from my cock, a stream of my creamy soup dripping from the corner of her lips. My wife seems rather ill after consuming my bollocks juice and just now I wonder if she might vomit upon me.

"Are you alright?" I ask while reaching for her hand once again.

"Fine," Lydia replies while breathing hard. "I am fine." She bats away my hands and I sit back with my wilting cock sitting outside my trousers. Pulling it inside, I quickly tuck it away so that the driver outside might not see it.

"Why did you do this to me?" I ask. "You have refused to do anything of the sort for our entire marriage, Lydia. What has changed?"

Her face deep red, she shakes her head. "I simply decided to do this for you," is her quick reply. "Did you enjoy it, Lewis?"

I chuckle. "Of course I enjoyed it, Lydia. The fact that you have done something utterly unlike you has not gone unnoticed, either."

Though I would like to hear from her why she has decided to bestow upon me the fellatic act, I get the sense my dearest wife will not explain herself to me. However, I do wonder if something about last night at the Hutchins's home has altered her perceptions as to what is acceptable or unacceptable in our marriage. It has always been my strongest view that so long as it is agreeable to both the husband as well as the wife, it cannot be outside morality. Even so, the moral repugnance Lydia has shown toward placing my phallus into her mouth even for a moment has been very strong before today. Something indeed has changed.

"We are to see them again soon," she tells me after several minutes. "Adelia and I have things to do."

"Things to do? Have you been speaking to her about our intimate life, Lydia?"

She turns her face to me. "Why would you ask such a thing, Lewis? Do you wish to embarrass me?"

"No, my love, I was just..."

"Is this because I have just given in to your depraved nature, husband? Have you decided that my willingness to give you such a thing as I have means that I have been sharing about our very secret times in bed with another woman? How could you believe such a thing?"

Lydia has suddenly become angry at me for making such an accusation, even if it were an innocent question so that I might better understand her current behavior. However, I find it difficult to carry on with this line of questioning as she shakes her head and continues ranting toward me.

"You should be ashamed of yourself, sir. I am your wife."

"I know you are, my lady, but..."

"Do not ever accuse me of such things again, Lewis. I am not a whore who takes lightly the things I do for my husband. Whatever I decide is most assuredly allowed, I will allow. There will be no others who convince me of their validity."

Nodding my head and sitting back in my seat, I decide to simply drop the entire thing. My indelicate questioning has caused a seething anger within my bride to come out. Though I thought my questions to be quite timid, Lydia does not perceive them in the same light. Therefore, I cannot continue with them. Not now and probably not ever again. At least, not unless I wish to cause her more upset.

We arrive home and I watch as my wife immediately walks into the house. The driver of the carriage looks at me in wonder as he helps me pull down a small bag Lydia had carried with her. After he tips his hat, the driver then turns the horses and carriage around before leaving our home. I walk inside and quietly go to change my clothes. Though I am not to be at the office today, a Saturday, I have promised to help a farmer nearby move several cattle to a nearby field. It pays a little, and I am not one to give up any money, no matter how small.

"Will you be gone all day?" Lydia asks as I prepare later to walk out the door.

"Until dark or a bit later," I reply as I hope for an embrace from my wife and possibly a kiss. Unfortunately, there is not one to be had before I open the door and leave our house. She is angry with me, and I am uncertain just why. It is not as if I have accused her of whoring, as she apparently believes. All I sought to know was what had happened to change her mind on allowing her mouth to pleasure me in such a way. Lydia does not wish to tell me, and so it will probably remain a mystery for a very long time.

Chapter Six: The Weight of the World

"Good Monday to you, sir!" Phineas says as he greets me just inside the office door.

"Good morning, sir," I reply with a smile on my face. "How are you this day?"

"Fine and happy," he says to me while putting a hand on my shoulder. "I have a gentleman to whom I would like to introduce you."

I walk with him into his office and find inside a middle-aged man sitting in a chair to one side. The aroma of his person is immediately off-putting, causing me to put my hand to my nose for a moment. However, my years of working on a farm have made me able to become quickly accustomed to such heinous assaults upon my olfactory senses.

"Mr. Colin O'Toole, this is the solicitor who shall be by your side in court. His name is Lewis Dabney."

The man stands to his feet, his somewhat worn clothing clinging to his smelly body as he does. He offers me his hand, and I accept it, though I begin to wish I had done something besides accepting this greeting.

"Honour to meet you, boy," he says to me. "There is much to discuss, eh?"

"Certainly there is," I agree with Mr. O'Toole as we all make ourselves more comfortable.

"Mr. Dabney was at the top of his coursework at university," Phineas tells the client. "I believe you will find that he is an excellent solicitor for your representation."

"Bollocks the magistrate," the older man chuckles. "Bollocks to him and to his wife."

"Mr. O'Toole, we have discussed these outbursts. They will not be so helpful to you in the presence of the magistrate."

"Eh, the man will be a shite pile," the accused vagrant says with a scowl upon his face.

"They are all shite, sir. I do not bow to shite."

"You must hold that tongue," I tell him firmly. "For your sake as well as for mine."

He turns to look at me, his blue-grey eyes studying my form for a moment before saying to me, "How old are ye, sir?"

"A score and five," I answer.

"Eh, I have clothes older than ye."

"The ones you are wearing, I would suppose?" I retort.

"Gentlemen," Phineas chuckles. "We must come to an agreement as to what must be done before the magistrate next week. You cannot go in whilst in a tussle with each other." After taking a breath, he asks me, "What would be your suggestion, Mr. Dabney? How should we proceed with Mr. O'Toole?"

I wish to say that the man first needs a very long bath in the Thames. However, I can see that such a remark would likely sour the relationship we already have as a client and solicitor. Seeing that I shall need to be the one to make the decision of how to proceed, I decide to offer a very direct idea.

"Plead guilty and for mercy before the court."

"Eh? Are ye out of yer gourd?" Mr. O'Toole shakes his head while frowning once again.

"You will not win this case," I say as I lean back into my seat. "The Vagrancy Law of 1847 allows the Crown to lay upon a person such as yourself a terrible price, Mr. O'Toole. If found guilty, you would be required to go to a workhouse for at least a year, if not longer."

"Workhouses are not so bad," he tells me. "They feed a man there."

"They do," I agree, "However, they also confine you, and I do not see a man such as yourself agreeable to confinement."

The man shakes his head. "What do ye know of me? I will be fed. That is all I care for."

"And they will require you to bathe and wear work clothes."

He leans toward me in his seat, the odour from his body more offensive due to this movement. "I will not bathe. 'Tis unsanitary."

Though I nearly laugh, I keep my composure as I continue, "They will force you to bathe at least once each week and possibly more. The masters of the workhouses do not allow any man to skip his responsibility to cleanliness."

Mr. O'Toole continues to frown, his lack of teeth making his face seem an even deeper caricature of himself.

"What must I do to rid myself of this?" he asks.

"You must become as a mouse in a church, good sir. Otherwise, you will surely see yourself in a bath five or six times each and every month."

There is a slight grin that begins to grow along the face of the other solicitor across the desk from me. Though Phineas asked for my suggestion as to what must be done, I believe this very idea is similar to what he might have suggested were he the solicitor working to help Mr. O'Toole in court. There is a sense of pride within me as I wait patiently to hear from my client as to what he thinks about my idea. He must accept it, or live with the fact that he will be forced to bathe occasionally.

"The government is insufferable," he tells me after a moment of thought. "They are the devil, they are."

"Perhaps so, but you must seek your own freedom, sir. I can only help to guide you toward it."

After some coaxing, he finally agrees, nodding his head and even smiling a bit. Phineas and I continue to speak with him about the great importance of keeping his mannerisms in check and speaking only when spoken to by the magistrate. It is the only way to help Mr. O'Toole, and it seems by the time he leaves our office that he understands this.

"He is a difficult man," Phineas offers after we see the client out of our office. "However, we have agreed to take him on due to Lady Elquist's insistence."

"Lady Elquist? Have I heard this name?"

"You likely have, but she prefers to remain in the shadows. Lady Elquist is funding this man's defence and that is why we have taken it on."

"Is she paying well?" I ask while raising an eyebrow.

"Not as well as someone who pays for their own defence, but she has seen a need for such things. Mr. O'Toole is a very blessed man, though he does not see it. His mind has gone too far for him to appreciate that which is given to him."

"Agreed," I reply. After some thought, I tell him, "My wife and I did very much appreciate the meal and drinks on Friday evening last."

"We enjoyed the visit," Phineas replies with a smile. "You were both very good guests."

"Yes. The visit has seemed to have a dramatic impact upon Lydia." I lick my lips as I look down at the papers on my desk. Though I have not intended this comment to pique Phineas's curiosity, it has apparently done as much.

"In what way?" he asks.

I look back up at him. "Well, it is difficult to explain, honestly. You see, my wife has never been the overly adventurous type when it comes to our marital relationship. She is shy."

"Quite shy," he affirms. "Lydia and I discussed this in the library late Friday evening into Saturday morning."

"Wait," I say as my mind processes what I have just heard. "You were with her at that time?"

"I was," he replies. "And we spoke for some time about her concerns and how you have worked so diligently in life to see that she is very happy."

My eyes look into Phineas's eyes and I wonder just what was said between the two of them. Why would she go to see him and speak to him about our very private life together? It seems a violation of some moral code for a woman to speak to another man in private without her husband's approval.

"What brought her to you?" I ask.

Phineas smiles. "I was in the library for a time while enjoying a late night brandy. I suppose Lydia saw the lamplight inside and decided to come in to speak to me. We did, and I must tell you that your wife is very outgoing when she decides she is safe."

"She has always been safe," I tell him. "Not once have I allowed another to cause her harm."

He shakes his head. "I do not think she fears for her life, Lewis. Instead, I believe Lydia to be worried about where your lives will go after you have become a very good solicitor."

Grimacing, I tell him, "Nothing will change. We will continue to be a very happy couple, sir."

"That is not what she told me," he replies. "In fact, she is concerned that you might falter in your promises to her."

My jaw drops slightly as I attempt to understand what I am being told. "Of which promises do you speak?"

Phineas shakes his head. "I have said too much already. Surely you think me to be a terrible cad for being so forthright, sir."

"Did she tell you I would not keep my vows to her?" I ask plainly. "Tell me, sir. I deserve to know if Lydia no longer sees me as a fit husband."

"She worries that you are going to find yourself with other women as you become more successful, and so she believes there might be one or more willing to give in to your desires more so than she has." He shakes his head. "It was never my intention to hear this from your wife when she came to the library, Lewis. Please do not think me the one to instigate our conversation."

My heart sinks deep into the pit of my stomach. I love Lydia so very much, yet at times I wonder how much more of her prudish behaviour I can take. She does not appear interested for the most part in seeing to having unbridled intercourse with me, and there have been times when I have considered how this affects my own relationship with her. Even so, I will never leave her and I will never stop loving her dearly. There is no other woman for me besides Lydia.

"Thank you for informing me of what she has spoken of to you," I reply. "Surely she will seek some solace in her new friendship with Adelia as well."

"She has already, Lewis. I believe they will be close friends, one to the other."

"Excellent." I offer a quiet smile before telling Mr. Hutchins, "I must take time to review Mr. O'Toole's case a bit more before I go to court with him next week. Hopefully he will remain on his best behaviour. Otherwise, I fear what the magistrate might do with him."

"He shall obey your every command," Phineas says while patting my shoulder. "I believe you have brought him into the light concerning what he must do, sir. You have a way with words when it comes to his sort of man."

"Perhaps that is not always the best thing. I have not lived as a vagrant, Mr. Hutchins."

"Ah, but you have a much different understanding of his type than most. Please, do not take this as a slight, Lewis. You have a gift that most of us can only wish we had." Phineas offers a smile once more before bowing his head slightly and leaving me to do my work.

What he has told me concerning my wife is a strange thing. Why would they have spoken alone in the library while I slept? Would that night cause some difficulties between him and his own wife? It is not exactly what would be the gentlemanly thing to do, as far as I am concerned. Though I am not upset with him for speaking with Lydia for meeting with her that night in the library, I do not like the appearance it offers. Hopefully he has seen my discomfort and will not allow my wife to speak with him alone in the same way again.

Chapter Seven: Secrets Abound

41

Lydia is not home after a long day of handling Mr. O'Toole's case in court. Though I had hoped to spare him a sentence in the prison or the workhouse, the old man managed to slight the magistrate several times, causing anger to be poured out upon him through a three-week detention in the prison. At least they will not require him to clean himself while there. I suppose I should count this aspect of his case a minor victory.

"Lydia?" I call out as I make my way through the small home. We only have the one bed chamber in the house, so it is not as if she might be elsewhere. As my concern increases, I walk out through the back door and into our small garden. No one is here, and I am beginning to worry for my dear wife. Where has she gone and why?

It is not until I go back into the house that I finally see a small note left on the kitchen table. Picking it up, I read it to myself.

"Don't worry, Lewis. I have gone to see a friend this evening. Should I return this same evening, I will of course come by carriage. You have no reason to be concerned. Lydia."

"A friend?" I say with confusion. "You have no friends nearby." Confused and worried, I leave our house and go a short distance down the road to visit our nearest neighbors, George and Clara Martin. When I arrive, I see Clara sweeping off the front porch. "Good evening, Clara."

"Oh. Hello, Lewis." She leaves the porch and walks over to the fence. "Where is your wife?"

I sigh. "She is not home at the moment. I thought I might come by to see if you know where she might have gone."

Her eyebrows raise. "Did she leave a note?"

"She did," I tell her. "It doesn't mention a place. She only says she has gone to see a friend."

"The one in Southampton?"

I shake my head as I look back at her. "Southampton? Has she said anything to you about a friend there? She has not told me as much."

"Of course. Lydia told me two days ago that she had met a friend last week while you were both there. If she is mentioning seeing a friend, could it be her?"

It all suddenly makes perfect sense to me. "Mrs. Hutchins. She has gone to see her."

"Is that her name?"

"I believe so, yes," I reply. "Thank you so much for letting me know, Clara. You have been very helpful."

"I do what I can, Lewis." She smiles before turning to go back to her work on the front porch. For my part, I turn and make my way back to our house and then go inside.

"Dammit," I mutter before sitting down in a chair at the kitchen table. "Why would you do this, Lydia?"

Before meeting the Hutchins for dinner last Friday evening, Lydia was not interested in becoming friendly with anyone. We had for years attempted to cultivate friendships with others, but it was quickly apparent that my wife was not cut out for such social endeavours. She has been shy and very slow to warm to people for as long as I have known her, and at times this quality has given us terrible issues with those we love and hold dear to us. Even our families do not feel close to Lydia whenever we visit them.

I sit quietly for some time while trying to figure out what I might do to make certain that Lydia has in fact gone to see Adelia. I do not want to make more of the fact that she is not here than I need to, but it is important that I know for certain she is safe.

"Dammit," I say again as I suddenly rise from my seat and take my coat before leaving the house. There is little daylight left and I must know what has happened to Lydia, no matter the consequences.

After visiting another neighbor, I borrow his horse and begin to travel to Southampton. I believe Lydia might be in the Hutchins home and I need to see this with my own eyes so that I will be satisfied as to her disposition for the evening. Of course, this would anger her completely if she knew I was seeking to keep an eye on her, but my wife is the world to me and I must see that she is safe at all times.

It takes me a half-hour to complete the journey before I tie the horse to a tree just outside of their property. Very quietly, I enter the open gate and walk down the short drive before getting to the main house. There are no servants standing outside, so I assume they have all gone to bed now that it is after seven o'clock in the evening. As a thief in the dark, I make my way around the perimeter of the home, peeking into the windows along the way.

My heart suddenly beats hard as I see my wife inside one of the lower rooms of the house. It appears to be the library, and she is completely nude, with a man lying beneath her. Just behind her sits Mrs. Hutchins with her breasts lifted out of her dress.

"Fuck," I mutter as I sit quietly outside the window. Though it takes a moment, I realize that the man lying beneath Lydia is none other than Phineas Hutchins. His cock is buried deep inside my wife's tight kitten as she moves up and down its length.

I can just make out the moans and other sounds from inside the room as the two of them make love together. Phineas reaches up and places his hands on each of her soft, round breasts and my dear wife smiles while her eyes are closed. She is enjoying the sensation of another man's hands upon her chest, and I feel jealous to see such a thing. Surely she has not given into this willingly. My wife would never do such a thing. Never.

"Why?" I say softly as I move closer to the window. "Where have you gotten such courage to do such a thing, Lydia? You will not even allow me to taste your sweet nectar."

Suddenly, I think back to last Saturday morning when my wife placed her mouth upon my cock and suckled it. That was the first time she had done such a thing for me, and it seemed almost miraculous that she had suddenly decided to do such a thing for me. However, it appears to have had a great deal to do with her conversation with Phineas earlier that morning. A conversation that probably looked very much like this one does now.

"Aaaahhhh..." I watch as Lydia's face becomes stretched into an expression of ecstasy. *"Ohhhhh..."* Her eyes open and for a brief instant our eyes meet before I drop back from the window. Has she seen me? I cannot be certain as I turn and run into the night and back to the horse.

As I reach the stallion, I hop onto its back and turn it to trot away. There are sounds of people's voices and I hear Lydia call out, "Lewis? Lewis, are you there?"

I dare not answer back. What I have seen is complete lunacy and beyond the comprehension of any other person who knows Lydia as well. Though I have had little reason before tonight to make such a charge, I begin to wonder whether she has lied to me about her fervent religious beliefs when it comes to what she is or is not willing to do in bed with me? It appears that there could be some validation for this concept. However, I will not confront her now to find out.

"Fucking wife!" I growl as I ride faster and faster down the road toward our home. Oh, that I might find Lydia there already! Surely it would be a better thing than I have seen already this evening. How she could go to have such intimacy with another man is beyond my understanding. I have worked on her behalf so long that I am uncertain whether what I have seen tonight is even real.

As I arrive back home, I tie up the horse for now and go to fetch him oats and water. The neighbor who allowed me to borrow the horse will not expect the horse back until the morning. So, I will keep the horse here for now instead of having to walk back in the dark. After situating the animal, I go into the house and sit down at the kitchen table. A stout drink of whiskey does some to settle my nerves as I consider what I have seen this evening.

Some time later, there is commotion outside the door of the house. Lydia soon walks into the house and looks at me quietly while standing nearby. She does not sit down, nor does she remove her cloak while keeping her hands folded in front of her.

"You have been gone for some time," I tell her with a deep frown. "Enjoying yourself, were you?"

Lydia looks at me and then down at the floor before looking back up again. "What did you see tonight, Lewis?"

"See *tonight?* It is pitch black outside, wife. What can a man see at this moment?" I refuse to give her the answer she wants from me.

"You know of what I speak," Lydia replies. "Have you been to their house, Lewis?"

"Whose house?"

"You know of which house I speak, my darling," she answers as if it does not bother her much at all. "Tell me the truth, Lewis. Where have you just now come from?"

"I have been here all evening," I lie confidently. "And you?"

Her eyes narrow slightly as she motions toward the door. "Why is there a horse tied outside, then? Have you not been to Southampton this night?"

I take a breath and glare at my wife. "You have been to Southampton, Lydia. Your friend is there, correct?"

Lydia swallows hard as she looks away briefly. Some part of her wants to hide away from me and declare that I did not see what I saw, but then another part wants to admit her naughtiness to me. I am curious to see what she is willing to say now that I have seen her with one of the men who agreed to my employment.

"You were there," she says to me quietly. "I did see you in that window, Lewis. I would swear to my life and then to my own mother's life. You watched us together."

My body shakes as if I have been placed into icy water. How do I answer such a declaration now that it is apparent that my wife has been fucking another man? What should I say?

"I was there, yes. You were on top of Mr. Hutchins and riding him quite nicely."

Her face turns deep red. "You were not supposed to know, Lewis."

"How was it that I was not to know?" I ask. "Did you really believe I would not think through what you said in your letter on the table? Lydia, I would hope that I am a better husband than that!" My anger begins to lift its ugly head as I continue staring at her. "Why do you fuck him?"

"Do not say it like that," she pleads with me.

"Like what? *Fuck?* Is that not what you did with him, my love? Surely it cannot be such a terrible thing to say when compared to what was done in reality."

"It is not a gentlemanly thing to say to a lady," Lydia tells me. "You should not speak in this manner to me."

Shaking my head, I say to her, "You *fucked* Phineas Hutchins. You *fucked* him hard." Sitting up straight, I then add, "Do you deny this at all?"

In her quiet voice while trembling, my wife tells me, "I do not deny it."

Nodding my head, I reply, "Then I shall sleep on the porch tonight. Good evening, Lydia." Walking toward the door, I retrieve a small blanket from a wooden box nearby. After going outside, I close the door and lie down on a wooden bench before covering myself with the blanket.

I will not sleep well outside in the cold air, but I doubt my ability to sleep at all this night regardless of what I do. The images of Lydia on top of Phineas Hutchins continue to fill my mind as I try to relax. There is little I can do to repair my marriage at this time. For now, I need to be away from her so that I can allow my mind to work through all that I know. Tomorrow will be another day. I will deal with the consequences of her actions at that time.

Chapter Eight: Coming Undone

48

"Please have something to eat," Lydia says to me as I get ready to leave to go to work. "You cannot just leave with an empty stomach, Lewis. It is not healthy."

"I am healthy enough," I reply without looking over at her. The aroma of eggs and blackened toast fill the small house, and I am very hungry already since I did not have dinner last night. Still, I have some principles and I refuse to allow myself to be wooed by my wife.

"Will you always hate me?" my wife finally asks as she sits down in a chair near the table.

"I do not hate you," I tell her.

"You do hate me, Lewis. I can see it on your face and by the way you refuse to have anything to eat. You are punishing me for what I have done."

There is some truth to what she says. Yes, I am angry at her for fucking another man the way she did, especially after refusing to allow me to enjoy her in more ways as her husband. Of course I want to make her feel terrible for what she has done, and there is little doubt in either of our minds that I am being quite successful at doing so. Even so, I still love my wife. I still care for her and want her to be completely happy, no matter what she has done to me. Then, why do I continue to be so rude to her this morning, two days after discovering what she has been up to with Phineas Hutchins and his wife Adelia?

"How many times have you been with him?" I ask.

She shudders. "You have asked me that thrice before and I have asked you to not ask me."

"And yet here I am, asking again," I reply dryly. "You owe me a response that is satisfactory, Lydia. After all, you have done what you swore never to do."

My wife shakes her head. "You will not allow me to go on past this, will you? I have promised to stay away from Phineas from now on, have I not? Must you know such things to satisfy yourself?"

"Yes, I must," I retort. "I must know how much fucking you have been handing out whilst refusing me something as simple as tasting of your quim."

"Lewis!" She recoils a little as she hears me speak of her nethers once again. "Be a gentleman."

"In the same fashion as Phineas Hutchins?" I snidely ask.

She shakes her head while frowning. "He is a gentleman, Lewis. The fact that you have your position should be evidence enough of that."

"Ah. Then you have been fucking him as a form of repayment for his magnanimity towards me?"

"You are so vile!" Lydie gets up and goes toward the wood stove where she had prepared breakfast. She quickly scrapes the food into a wooden bowl to be tossed out to our dog in the backyard later.

"I have not been intimate with any other woman," I tell her as I put my hand on the back of one of the chairs in the kitchen. "Not once have I looked at and lusted after another woman, either. For the last few years, I have been willing to go along with your wishes to not entertain such thoughts as spilling my seed or pleasuring you without copulation. And yet, I see no value in this at this point. All I know is that you have allowed another man to freely spread his seed upon your fertile ground."

"How would you know whether he put his seed inside me," she asks.

I chuckle. "I could smell it on you as soon as you walked back into our house that night, Lydia. It's not as if every man doesn't know what it smells like."

My cock growing a little, I turn to pick up my coat from a hook nearby. Though I do not see her staring at me, I feel as if I can feel my wife's eyes staring at me from behind. I have caused her pain, of course, just as she has caused me to wonder what it is a man must do to get his wife to fuck him like she would fuck another man. There was passion on her face as she enjoyed Phineas's cock buried inside her soft woolen lips. Had she not seen me outside the window, I might have remained quiet and continued to watch to see what else they might do with each other.

"I don't know what else to say to you," she says quietly. "I have asked for your forgiveness already, yet you will not give it."

"There is no reason to go out of my way to forgive you," I reply brusquely. "You did what you did without asking my thoughts on it and then you have refused to tell me how many times you allowed another man to put his cock inside you, Lydia. How can I forgive you for what you will not be honest about?"

She huffs. "Three times, alright? Phineas has released inside me three damned times. Is that what you want to hear?"

My cock becomes completely stiff as I hear her admit this to me. Covering my crotch with my coat, I turn to look at her. "Three times he spilled his bollocks' seed into you? Did you like it, Lydia?"

"What?"

"Did you like it? Was it something you would like to do again?"

Her face, already red, turns even deeper red as I quiz her on this point. "I don't know."

"You don't know?"

"I have sworn to you that I will not go back to him now that you know, but I cannot lie and say I would never do it again if allowed to do so."

"Fuck's sake."

"There you say it again!" Lydia shakes her head and grits her teeth. "Why do you treat me as if I have no value to you, Lewis? Why do you wish to say such things in my presence?"

I have used such vulgarity in my wife's presence more times in the last two days than all the years we have been married combined. Something about seeing her with another man has loosed my tongue, and I feel no remorse for behaving in such a terrible way. On the contrary, I feel as if I have some duty to continue saying such things around Lydia now that I know she was enjoying the presence of another man's cock inside her. What else am I to say? Do I conversate with her as if nothing has happened? Do I simply ask her to refrain from her bad behaviour in the future without giving her hell for it? I am angry, though not as much as I let on. There are some portions of what I now know that actually excite me in ways that are surprising.

"What shall I do with us?" I ask her calmly. "You have disgraced me by going to another man to do things with him you swore you would not do with me. So, what now?"

Lydia takes a breath and says, "I do not know the answer to this question. You are angry at me, which I do understand, but you also worry me by the way you seem so dismissive of me now. Has the love you had for me all these years suddenly subsided, Lewis?"

"I still love you dearly," I admit. "But I do not know what to do with what I now know. Things have been done that clearly paint you in a far different light from what I would have thought about you not long ago. How I move on from that, I do not rightly know."

We stand in the little house and stare at each other for a minute or two before I turn around and leave. There is a long ride ahead of me between here and the solicitor's office, and I need to get started now if I am to arrive in time.

"Your horse, Mr. Dabney," a young man says as he finishes brushing the brown coat of an animal I have not seen before.

"From where has this come?" I ask as I look at the handsome horse.

"Mr. Hutchins sent it for you. He says to keep the horse while you work in Southampton."

"Which Mr. Hutchins?" I ask for clarification.

"I do not know," he answers. "All he told me was to bring this horse to this house and he would pay me. That is all I know."

The lad hands me the reins of the horse before turning and untying another one from a post nearby. He then gets onto that horse and rides away toward Southampton. I am left with an animal that might be an attempt to buy off my anger toward Phineas after catching him with Lydia two nights ago.

"Damn him," I say under my breath before taking my satchel and lashing it to the new saddle of the horse. Putting one foot into a stirrup, I am soon on top of the animal and turning him toward Southampton. As I begin to trot away, I turn back for a moment to see my wife standing on the front porch of our small country home. There are things that still must be said between us, but this morning is not the time to do so. Instead, I must see to my work at the solicitor's office as well as to the man who has bedded my wife three times without my knowledge or permission. Surely this will be an interesting day, indeed.

Chapter Nine: None Are Hopeless

I walk into the office and turn to look at the door that normally leads to Phineas Hutchins' own desk and chair. For now, the lamp is not lit inside and the blinds are closed. The man has not shown up for work as of yet.

"Good morning, Lewis," James Hutchins says to me from his office door. "Would you please come have a seat inside?" He turns and goes back inside. I follow as well, putting down my satchel nearby before sitting down.

"Is your cousin to be late?" I enquire.

"He will not be along today," James answers with a nod. "However, I think you suspected as much when you noticed his office unoccupied."

"Does he feel ill?" I prod.

"He is concerned," James begins to explain. "There is apparently reason for him to be concerned, I take it?"

"Sir?"

James leans onto his elbows, his eyes looking into mine. "You may be forthright here, Lewis. There are no repercussions for saying what you must."

"Alright, then," I say after righting myself in my chair. "He has committed a great act against my wife and he needs to answer for it."

"A great act? Heavens, what has Phineas done?"

Grimacing, I reply, "You already know, do you not?"

James smiles. "I have been told that you saw my cousin with your wife in a very compromising position two days ago. Is that correct?"

"A *compromising position?* I believe I would label what I saw a bit more succinctly than that, sir."

"Of course." He sits back in his chair and shakes his head. "I am afraid that much of what has happened can be drawn back to me and what I have been about with my wife, Emma. You see, Phineas has taken some advice from me and I believe he has been acting upon it along with his wife."

"You told him to take Lydia to bed with him?" I ask with confusion.

"Not exactly, no. Instead, I encouraged him to enjoy many other things in the bedchamber with his wife than what most others would enjoy. You see, they are very much like me and my wife in that they share themselves with others."

"What a concept! Simply whore another man's wife for the sport of it," I say sarcastically. "Seems a wonderful thing, honestly. I'm grateful for knowing that Lydia has been brought into this fun they are having."

"Please, sir, I am attempting to explain."

"Ah, yes, you are explaining," I say to him while snarling a little. "Of course, I have yet to hear from your cousin directly concerning his violation of her honour."

I watch as James sighs and then gets up from his seat. What I have said has bothered him in some way, though I am uncertain as to which part bothers him most. There is no doubt that a question of honour is raised when one man violates another man's wife in such a way. My honour has been put into question, as has that of my wife.

"We do not see it as a question of honour, sir. In fact, we see it as simply a very natural thing that happens between men and women when they are in need of the touch of another. My cousin is very much like me in that respect, and I believe his willingness to give in is now due in some part to what I have said to him in the past. Please, if you wish to hold a deep grudge against another man, hold it against me. Phineas has learned some of what he knows from what I have told him."

"Did you put your dick inside my wife's quim?" I ask snarkily.

"No, I did not," he answers me with a chuckle.

"Then you are not the one with whom I hold a quarrel." I turn and leave his office to return to my desk. As I do, I can hear his footsteps not far behind. It appears Mr. Hutchins is not ready to release me from our conversation just yet.

"Please, do not be so hasty as to refuse to consider your new position," he advises me. "There are great benefits to the both of you should you decide to accept what has been given to you, Lewis."

Shaking my head, I ask, "What, pray tell, has been given to me?"

James sits down in a chair near my desk and takes a breath before answering, "Your wife is a lovely woman, is she not? Of course such a thing would be noticed by another. As it stands, there was something about Phineas and Adelia that also appealed to your wife, as otherwise she would not have so willingly participated with them that night."

There is a calmness to the way this man presents his cousin's case to me, almost as if he is the other's solicitor before the magistrate. Tempting as it might be to allow his sweet words to tickle my ears longer, I am becoming somewhat perturbed by the way he speaks to me as if I am some student who is in need of educating.

"Stop, please," I say while crossing my arms across my chest. "My wife is not some woman who was made for the jollies of another man. She is married to me and we hold vows. It is completely against Her Majesty's laws to commit adultery in this country, James. I assume your cousin is aware of as much?"

The gentle expression upon the man's face suddenly becomes much harder as he looks into my eyes. "Are you suggesting you would seek charges to be brought against the lot of them?"

"Against Phineas, yes," I confirm.

"No, it would be against all three, I am afraid. The law does not distinguish between the man or the woman when it comes to adultery, Lewis. You would be damning your own wife if you attempt to seek revenge in this way against my cousin."

Angry, I rise to my feet and look down at my employer. "Why have you brought me here, then? Was it to allow Phineas to plant his pecker firmly inside my wife? Did you plan with him such a plot to conjure up a time for them to meet and then fuck?"

"Your tongue, sir, is biting."

"And your cousin is a man whore who seeks women of lower class to simply use them for their honeypot." My rebuttal is stinging and at first I fully expect to be released from my duties at the solicitor's office.

However, James soon raises one eyebrow and begins to laugh at what I have said.

"A man whore," he roars with laughter. "I shall have to tell Phineas of his new title. Man Whore, esquire."

"'Tis not humorous," I tell him with some disdain for how James is reacting to my complaints.

"Of course it is, lad. Why have you become so downtrodden over such a minor thing? Surely you can see the benefits to be had here?"

"Benefits?"

"Aye, benefits." He gets up from his seat and walks over to me. "It is my theory that you have already lusted after the quim of my dear cousin's wife already."

"Sir!"

"Do not be so coy, Lewis. We both understand well what it is that you truly wish to have. Let me confirm to your own ears that Adelia can be yours just as your Lydia has allowed Phineas to breed her."

My cock swells momentarily as I hear these things from my employer's lips. Never before has another person told me that I am free to fuck another woman. Not once have I thought it possible to bed someone of the likes of Adelia Hutchins, either. However, James tells me such a thing is within my reach should I dare to grasp at it. What would this mean, then, if I accepted this quest? Would Adelia willingly give herself to me in the same way my wife has given herself to the likes of Phineas Hutchins?

"You say this, but it is a vile thing you propose."

"I propose that all involved would be happy should you decide such a course of action to be within your interests, sir. My cousin is quite willing to allow you to enjoy the pleasures of his wife in exchange for continuing to fill Lydia's sweet void."

My stomach retches a bit as I hear him say this in such a way, but at the same time I grow aroused by the thought of sliding into Adelia Hutchins's soft canyon. Surely it would be a wonderful sensation to know that woman in the carnal sense as I would release my seed deep inside her. Still, it would be an affront to the vows made between Lydia and I and I am not certain that is what I would prefer to do.

"This is madness," I say in a softer tone, my anger waning. "Complete madness."

"Yes, sir, it can be somewhat maddening at first. However, you will find that there are many wonderful experiences to be had if you but give in to it. Of course, this is the sort of understanding that only a man and his wife might have betwixt them, but I believe it is one that will meet to your liking all the same."

I consider what he is saying and find that I am conflicted at this point. There is truth in what James has said about me wishing to fill Adelia's quim with my cock. There is also truth in my thoughts that tell me I long to see Lydia skewered by her lover once again. Am I such a terrible husband to admit such a thing, even if only within the confines of my own thoughts?

"Phineas should be here to discuss such things as a man," I tell him.

"He is in court, good sir," James chuckles. "Did you think he would avoid you due to what you have seen? Of course he would not."

I nod my head. "We shall speak on this matter and I shall consider what you have said to me. For now, I am not willing to continue speaking of this, James. Not now."

"Of course." He bows his head slightly and smiles before turning and going back to his own office. After he closes the door, I sit back in my seat and shake my head.

"Absolute madness," I grumble while looking at the front door of the main office. I am not certain what I would do should the other Mr. Hutchins suddenly walk in. There is still anger within me, though much blunted now compared to earlier. Perhaps I will take seriously the words of the man who is here with me and think on what benefits might be afforded a man in my lowly standing. Shall I take to Adelia's beaver and mount her with the lusts of my flesh? Or shall I take up for the honour of my wife as well as my own. I cannot be certain which I will choose just yet. There is too much to consider to settle upon one thought so soon.

Chapter Ten: A Greater Understanding

61

"You are too wounded, my love. Please do not go." Lydia looks with grave concern at me as I gather a few things for the trip. "Do not go to see them."

I turn to look back at her. "You are welcome to come along if you are so worried about my safety, dearest wife." Lifting my satchel, I turn to go to the door.

"Dammit, Lewis! Why are you making so much of a very small thing?"

Stopping at the door, I make a fist in my empty hand and shake my head. "A very small thing? Surely you do not see what you have done with him a *very small thing,* my love?"

"It was just a moment in time between two people, my dear. I have not forsaken you nor have I forgotten our vows."

Turning, I ask, "Then what have you done? Do you not feel as if you have taken something away from our marriage?"

Lydia frowns. "I still love you and want to spend my entire life with you. Of course I do not feel that we have had something taken away."

"But, you have done that which you would not do with me!"

"We have been intimate many times, Lewis."

"Ah, but not in the ways I have asked," I retort. "You have allowed him to taste your quim, have you not?" I watch as her face turns deep red after asking this question of her. I must admit, there is a certain level of arousal on my part to see her consider the posit.

"Yes, Lewis, I have."

"Yet, I have done no such thing with you, my own wife." Shaking my head, I tell her, "Then what if I wish to taste the buttered valley of another woman? Would that be the sort of thing to which you would agree?"

Lydia's face becomes strained. "You would not do such a thing, Lewis. I know you well enough to know this."

"And I thought I knew you as well." After taking a deep breath, I turn and open the door before leaving our house. While walking to the carriage waiting for me, I can hear my wife's hurried footsteps. She does not intend to allow me to leave so easily without her.

"Wait, sir! I will come."

I turn and after seeing her face nod my head. My wife goes back into the house to retrieve her shawl and bonnet before returning. I offer her my hand and help her into the carriage before instructing him to take us to Southampton. Nodding his head, he shakes the reins just after I get into the carriage.

The ride is a silent one for the two of us. Lydia does not speak to me and I do not speak to her. There is resentment as well as a smattering of pride that fills the confines of the carriage between us, and I cannot decide how to address such a thing. Perhaps I have been altogether too severe in my assessment of what has happened between my wife and the other man, but then again I am wounded by such a thing. Hate is an ugly thing, so I attempt to dissuade it from becoming paramount in my thoughts toward Phineas Hutchins. Before pronouncing my thoughts on the matter, I have decided to allow him to speak about what he has done with my wife. We shall see what excuses manifest from his mouth.

We arrive at their home and Lydia is first helped out of the carriage by the driver before I hop out just behind her. My wife and I approach the front door of the large house and a smartly dressed man opens the door for us. He waves a hand toward the open doorway and we walk in, apparently expected by the occupants this day.

"Hello, Mr. and Mrs. Dabney. Please follow me." Another man inside the doorway turns and leads the two of us toward the parlor nearby. Once we are inside, he quietly closes the double doors and we are left alone.

"Do not say anything you will regret," Lydia quietly pleads with me. "He is still your employer, Lewis."

"One-half of my employer," I remind her. "James is not so caustic towards me after our conversation."

"Still, you must show some reserve, husband. Do not threaten either of them, I beg you. You are the better man, Lewis. I tell you this because I love you and I wish to remain your wife for many more years." Lydia puts her hands into mine as I stand and stare at the doorway. I do not want to miss the grand entrance of the man who filled my wife's furry pussy with his spunk.

Some minutes go by before the doors open. In walk both Phineas and his wife Adelia, smiles on both of their faces.

"Good afternoon, Lewis," Phineas says as she extends a hand to shake.

"Forgive me, but I do not see the point," I tell him. He drops his hand, a look of disappointment spreading across his face.

"You are angry," he notes. "Lewis, I do completely understand. I have been in exactly the same situation in which you currently find yourself."

"He has," Adelia offers as she approaches me. "Please know that this was not intended to be so difficult for you. It was our intention to bring you into our little fold once Lydia felt it was time."

"Your *fold?* What do you mean by this?" I ask.

She approaches me slowly, reaching up just as she gets close enough that I am able to smell the perfume on her body. My cock snaps to attention inside my trousers as she runs her fingers along my cheek and then my ear. What witchery is this that she applies to me?

"You are a fine young man," Mrs. Hutchins tells me. "It is our hope that in time you will see things as we have come to see them. Your wife wishes the same as well." Lydia smiles as she looks into my eyes. "Do you not wish to see Lydia with my husband again?"

"What?" I feel my body giving in to the whims of this vixen before me.

"It is only natural to want for someone else, Lewis. We do not act to leave our marriages, you see. We act to enjoy more fully those things in this life that we should not be allowed to have. Our lusts are thick as we seek out those who are very much like us."

Adelia takes my hand and leads me to a couch. We sit down as she keeps her eyes on me. For a moment, I do not notice what is happening between the other two people in the room. However, my curiosity gets the better of me and I turn to see my wife and Phineas kissing passionately. My cock, excited by the sudden sight, grows even more. The woman in the seat beside me can feel this change in girth and length as her thigh rests against it outside my trousers.

"Let me have a peek," she says as she reaches for the front of my trousers.

"Only one woman besides my mother has seen it," I tell her. "You must understand, I try to be a gentleman at all times. Though I know I am not socially your equal, I work to become what I am not."

She smiles at me as she unfastens my trousers. "We are friends, sir. Allow me this honour." Adelia works her hand inside and finds my hardness awaiting her. Pulling gently, she fishes it out of its dark confines and out into the light so that she might look it over. "You have a magnificent cock, Lewis."

"My lady," I say as I breathe hard. "You cannot do this."

"Do what?" Adelia bends down and kisses the tip of it before parting her lips and allowing it to slide into her mouth. The sensation of the action is incredible as I feel my bollocks tense inside my trousers.

"Oh, Phineas," my wife moans as he pulls at her dress to expose her soft breasts. Though I wish to leap to my feet to stop the man from having at my wife, I cannot. His wife's soft lips are caressing the sides of my thick cock.

For the next several minutes, Lydia undresses and kisses her lover as he does the same. Adelia quietly continues suckling at my hardness until suddenly, I explode.

"*Naaaahhhhh...AAAHHHHH!!!*" I expect to see her lift her head immediately to keep from having my seed fill her mouth, but Adelia does not. Instead, she hungrily swallows each powerful spurt from the end of my hard manhood. Never before have I had another woman eat my meaty shaft and then swallow the contents from within. The experience, in my estimation, is life-changing. *"OOOOHHHH!!! OOOOHHHH!!!"*

Adelia slides her mouth away from my cock once I have finished and then stands to her feet to remove her dress. My cock, though flaccid at this point, begins to show signs of life once again as I take in the beauty of her body. The woman is wholly involved in having me as she wants me this afternoon, and I am powerless to stop her.

"Fuck! *FUCK!!!*" Phineas wedges his very girthy member deep into Lydia's beaver as he pushes her legs back against her chest on another couch nearby. *"FUCK!!!"* He fucks her deeply, the end of his fleshy spear stabbing into the end of my wife's cave. The man intends to have my wife in his own way, no matter the words from her mouth.

"My sweet lover," Phineas moans as he slaps her arse hard. "You are so delicate. I cannot wait to fill you completely with my own sauce." The sound of his balls slapping Lydia's arsehole is incredibly loud as he has his way with her.

"Come to me," Adelia says as she spreads her legs and pulls them back to reveal her trimmed creature. I go to my knees on the floor between her legs and she tells me, "You have wanted to taste one, have you not? Taste of mind, Mr. Dabney. Tell me what you think of what I offer." She giggles as I look at her glistening light-brown hairs. I can smell her sweet aroma within my nostrils as I near her quim. My cock fully engorges as I lean forward and press my mouth to her wetness.

"Oh, fuck, Phineas!" I hear Lydia moaning behind us. Her pleas with the lover on top of her becomes more distant as I push my tongue into Adelia's tasty hole. The sweetness of her snatch is incredibly satisfying and I want so much more.

"Move up a little," she pleads with me. "There! That spot!" A small nub is hidden within the hairs of Mrs. Hutchins's wooly muffin. I take it into my lips and pull at it as my tongue moves quickly across it. "Oh, fuck, sir! Fuck, you've found it!" Her body shudders with enjoyment as I continue working with the swelling part. "Oh, Lewis!" Her hands move to my head and she pulls at me as I enjoy pleasuring her.

There is a great deal of noise within the room as my wife and her lover continue making love. I hear them both moan loudly at times, and I can only imagine that Phineas is seeding Lydia's fertile garden as I feast upon his own wife. Though I was before very cross with all three of them, I am now happy as I give Adelia something I have not given another woman before.

"Ooooohhhh...OOOHHHH!!! FUCK!!! LEWIS!!! FUCK!!!" She keeps her fingers inside the hairs of my head, pulling me hard against her nethers. My lips and tongue continue to work hard for her as I wish to make Adelia as happy with what I am able to do as my wife is with Phineas. *"AAAAHHHH!!! OHHHHH!!!"*

We continue in this way for several hours, Adelia once again sucking my cock and I filling her mouth with me seed as Phineas releases into my own wife's mouth. I now see where it was that Lydia got her inspiration to do the same for me a few days ago.

"Marvelous!" Phineas says as he sits back on the couch to catch his breath. "Everything is marvelous!"

"And you, sir?" Adelia asks me. "What is your opinion?"

"You are very pleasant to taste," I say while blushing.

"As are you," she replies with a wink.

Turning my eyes toward Lydia, I ask, "Was this what you wanted, my dear? To see me with another woman?"

"Perhaps," she replies. "I wanted more to be with Phineas again, I must admit. However, you and I shall be as close as ever, my love. I swear it."

Smiling at her, I reply, "I swear it as well, Lydia. No matter what we shall do together from now on, it will be with each other."

I am beginning to understand all that James told me yesterday concerning what his cousin was up to when it came to my wife. Phineas and Adelia have wished to see me come with Lydia to their home and enjoy them altogether. There was no crafty thought to take her from me, but instead they wished to experience us together. I am happy to have finally given in, though I do wish things had been done differently in many ways so as to avoid confusion. Even so, the tenor of the room is one of happiness and satisfaction. Certainly, I cannot hope for more.

Chapter Eleven: New Opportunities and Problems

"You do me the honour to be my husband," my wife says as we look over the small garden behind our home.

"And you have done me a great honour as well," I tell her. "Very much so and in all ways."

She raises an eyebrow. "You would have only a week ago not said so, Lewis. Have you already forgotten?"

I chuckle. "No, I have not. Still, you have convinced me that there are many other things we can do together that we did not do before. If only my skull had been a bit thinner, I might have much earlier given in to what you were about."

"Mr. Dabney?" I hear a voice call out to us from nearby. There is a man standing on the other side of our fence while waving at us. Lydia and I make our way toward him so that we might see what is the matter.

"Hello, sir. Who might you be?"

"Thank heavens you are here," he replies. "I am Sir Robert Clarke, a close friend of the Hutchins families as well as their occasional counsel."

"Hello sir." I reach over and shake the older man's hand. "To what do we owe the pleasure of your visit?"

His face is sullen, almost sad as he hands me an envelope. "These are tickets for passage to Norway, sir. Oslo, that is."

"Norway?" I open the envelope and reach inside to see two tickets and lengthy instructions on a sheet of paper. "What is this about?"

"Phineas and Adelia are in certain trouble," he tells me. "I fear they may find themselves detained at the moment in Oslo."

"Detained? Why are they in Oslo?"

He sighs and shakes his head. "It was against my better counsel, but they will do only what it is they think is necessary whether it is wise or not. You see, Mrs. Hutchins's father is in Oslo and the authorities there have taken him into custody over what should have been a very small matter. Unfortunately, the matter has grown and now it is an international scandal. You must go there and seek to have them freed to return."

"Me?"

"And your wife," he tells me. "Adelia has asked for her since she was taken into the prison there."

"Prison?" Lydia shakes her head as she begins to cry. "We cannot allow them to remain there, Lewis! We must go!"

"And you?" I ask him. "You are obviously the more experienced solicitor. Why are you not going?"

He shakes his head. "I am barred from entering the country, as is James at this time. The only other ones Phineas and his wife trust are the two of you."

"Fuck," I mutter as I shake my head. "I've never been outside of England. Not even to Scotland."

"It is your time to spread your wings, then, sir," Sir Robert tells me. "They need you desperately and I am afraid there may not be much time. The magistrate there is keen on seeing them all in prison for a decade or longer."

"For what?" I ask.

"Oh. You have not heard." He shakes his head. "Phineas and Adelia attempted to free her father from prison. He was arrested for some sort of misunderstanding concerning his work there as a merchant."

"Shite."

I have heard the story from James not too long ago as to how Phineas and his wife saved her father from a long prison time in England only to send him to Norway. If he has been arrested again for the same crime in another country, this will not be an easy thing to defend against. Surely his daughter's plight and that of Phineas will be difficult as well. I have no understanding of Norwegian law, so my capabilities will be severely limited.

"We must go," Lydia tells me as she squeezes my arm. "We will pack immediately."

I nod my agreement just before my wife goes into the house. Looking at Sir Robert, I ask, "What advice do you have for me, sir? Surely you can tell me what it is I must do once I arrive."

He sighs. "Be careful what you say to those in the courts there, Mr. Dabney. They are quick to accuse and slow to forgive in Norway's courts. Be respectful, yet firm as you propose your defense of them. Above all, show no fear. From what I remember of my short time visiting there, the magistrates there enjoy stirring fear and doubt in foreigner's minds. They will test you, but you must remain strong."

"Aye. Thank you for that," I tell him. "We will go to port as soon as we are ready."

"A carriage will be awaiting you," Sir Robert replies before turning to leave the fence line. I watch as he mounts another carriage nearby before going into the house to help my wife prepare to leave.

"We cannot leave them there," Lydia says with grave concern. "They are terrible people, the Norwegians."

I chuckle. "They are not, my love. I believe we will be able to gain their freedom once we arrive and discuss with them what has surely been misperceived by those in authority in Oslo."

"Misperceived? Lewis, you did hear Mr. Clarke, did you not? He says Phineas and Adelia were involved in a plot to break her father out of the prison there. Why would they risk such a thing? It is a terrible thing to do and they have now found themselves at the mercy of the Norwegian courts."

I reach toward my wife and gently pull her to me. "Do not fear this thing, my love. We will go and plead our case to those in authority there and in doing so they will see that none of them should be imprisoned. Have faith in me, my love." I kiss Lydia before turning to pack my own bag for the trip.

"I am very sorry, Lewis. You are right to ask me to trust you. For all it might be worth, I wish you to know that I see you with great admiration and I trust you wholeheartedly, my dear. Do not ever forget that I love you above all else and I would gladly follow you to whatever ends there would be."

"There will only be their freedom once we have explained our side of the argument, Lydia," I tell her with a smile upon my face. "All will be well. Wait and see."

TO BE CONTINUED

TO BE CONTINUED IN PART 2

Did you love *Hot Wife Game - A Victorian England Hotwife Wife Watching Romance Novel*? Then you should read *Hotwife For Hire - A Western Historical Era Hotwife Wife Watching And Wife Sharing Contemporary Romance Novel*[1] by Karly Violet!

[2]

From Barmaid To Lady For Hire' In Texas 1879!

In the dusty town of Saddleback Ridge, Texas, 1879, young couple William and Lila leave their Tennessee roots behind with dreams of a better life.

Despite their love and determination, this passionate pair struggles to make ends meet.

By day, William works as a bank teller, while Lila serves drinks at the town bar - Faded Rose.

---

1. https://books2read.com/u/mVDOGl

2. https://books2read.com/u/mVDOGl

But when a tempting offer leads Lila upstairs to the rooms of 'whores for hire', their lives take an unexpected turn.

With her husband's consent, Lila embraces this risqué opportunity, and the couple embark on a journey stretching the boundaries of their marriage.

As William watches his wife's secret trysts through a hidden hole in the wall, they find themselves attracting the attention of Saddleback Ridge's influential elite.

Loyal husband watches as his beautiful wife shares her body with the powerful aristocrats!

Discover the intrigue, passion, and ambition of a sexually adventurous married couple in the wild west in this tantalizing 20,000 word tale that explores the lengths one couple is willing to go to.

Read more at https://www.patreon.com/karlyviolet.

Printed by Libri Plureos GmbH in Hamburg, Germany